THE MAMMOTH BOOK OF
Illustrated
Erotica

THE MAMMOTH BOOK OF
Illustrated
Erotica

EDITED BY MAXIM JAKUBOWSKI & MARILYN JAYE LEWIS

CARROLL & GRAF PUBLISHERS

NEW YORK

Carroll & Graf Publishers
An imprint of Avalon Publishing Group, Inc.
245 W. 17th Street
11 th Floor
New York
NY 10011-5300
www.carrollandgraf.com

First published in the UK in 2001 by Robinson,
an imprint of Constable & Robinson Ltd

First Carroll & Graf edition 2001
Fourth printing 2003

ISBN 0-7867-0921-9

Design and layout by Design Revolution Limited.
Printed and bound in the EU.

PHOTOGRAPH CREDITS

Title page: Benjamin Hoffman
Imprint page: Jorge Parra
Contents page: Maurizio Mauri
Page 8: Marc Travanti; page 9: Harry Wynn; page 10: Veretta; page 11: Roger Tassin

CONTENTS

INTRODUCTION

Following the success of the first five volumes of THE MAMMOTH BOOK OF EROTICA, which have been instrumental in expanding the popularity of erotic writing, we are pleased to be taking the imprint into another dimension with this massive compendium featuring some of the best erotic photography from around the world.

Ever since people began writing stories, depictions of sex and relationships have formed an integral part of fiction. Likewise, since the invention of photography, representations of the human body and sexuality have proven an irresistible subject for photographers and for the voyeurs in all of us.

The desire to bring an impressive collection of talent under one cover at an affordable price has always been one of the fundamental principles of the Mammoth series, so it seems apt that our first

venture into the field of visual arts should offer a fascinating selection of nude and erotic photography. The work of almost 80 photographers from a wide variety of countries and backgrounds have been gathered for this ground-breaking collection. We are proud to provide exposure not only to some of the best-established and recognized photographers in the field, but also to introduce many up and coming talents.

The body and its secrets and taboos is at the heart of human sexuality, and its representations in art can vary enormously. By witnessing the body in its ultimate and vulnerable reality, the camera never lies. Or can it? How is it that every body is different and that canons of corporal beauty can differ so much from individual to individual, from race to race, country to country, and era to era. Who is to say that the often pear-shaped nudes of the early 20th century are any less erotic than today's stick-thin models or the Rubenesque matrons of centuries past? Are blurred, sometimes almost abstract images of bodies, where the flesh rises from the darkness like primeval mud or loses its sharpness to make way for soft shapes and sensuous curves any more or less titillating than realistic close-ups where every mole, blemish or sexual feature stands out proudly? As ever, eroticism is very much in the eye of the beholder.

What defines eroticism is as unique to each photographer as it is to each viewer. While photographers might share tastes as far as an erotic genre – fetish for instance, with its emphasis on certain features or the ritual element of clothing or lack of it surrounding the flesh and body – each photographer has his or her unique way of capturing that genre and bringing a fresh eroticism to the subject.

With more than 500 photographs, this book presents a dazzling panorama of poses, shapes, angles and nudes in all their splendour. Not one is alike and, should any of the attractive models herein have been photographed by all 80 of our photographers, each representation would be very different. He or she would be different for each photographer and shown as such: the key to the image is not just the body or body part on show, but also the way the photographer views his or her model, the setting and the mood. A photographer's choice of location is often as entertaining as the subject. For instance, look at the Motel Fetish photos of Chas Ray Krider, the use of outdoor settings by Adam Butler, or the use of Italian ruins and landscapes in the work of Maurizio Mauri, which juxtaposes decay against a seemingly delicate female nude.

Some of our contributors frequently make use of their own bodies as subjects or canvases. Some, like Petter Hegre with his fascinating

photographs of his wife, use their loved ones, while others prefer the anonymity of amateur models, exhibitionists or professionals. But the fascination for the sexuality that bodies exude remains paramount; the bodies on display here evoke the mysteries of sexuality, desire and lust as much as the sheer formal beauty of the human form, and that is what constitutes the very essence of eroticism.

Some of the photographers included here exclusively use the erotic medium. Others have already established a name for themselves in entirely different media, and erotica is just one facet of their work. Others, such as Julie Strain and Jody Frost started as models and are now breaking into the erotic photography genre. But all the photographers display a major talent for the form and we are proud to include them. Next to film-making, photography is probably the most expensive medium for an artist to undertake. Thanks to the Internet, it is now easier for a photographer's images to reach a much wider audience relatively cheaply. While putting this book together, we found the Internet and a variety of specialist sites and web magazines proved invaluable in helping us discover and reach photographers internationally, so we could feature artists whose work we might not have been aware of otherwise.

Many of the more established photographers that we have included in this collection were licensed through the invaluable help of Nicky Akehurst. We owe Nicky a big vote of thanks for believing in the project and, where necessary, pleading our cause and justifying our limited budgets. We are also grateful to everyone who recommended photographers to us, particularly Abby Ehman.

There are, of course, some photographers that we were not able to include in the book for various reasons, although both of us are great fans of their work. We can only hope that we will have the opportunity to include them in a book in future.

In the meantime, enjoy this wonderful collection of nudes and erotic images. Be dazzled, turned on, amazed and know that there is no end to the beauty of the human form.

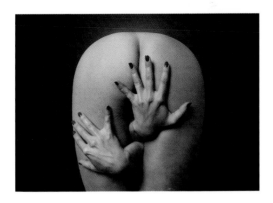

HENRIK AGELBY

Henrik Agelby was born in 1963 in Copenhagen. Since 1983 he has worked full-time in the insurance business. He took up photography in 1990, and in 1992 some of his erotic images were selected for an exhibition at Copenhagen's Erotic Museum. He has since worked for various magazines on a freelance basis and had his first exhibition in a local art gallery in 1993. Henrik has subsequently had his photographs included in magazines around the world.

SARAH AINSLIE

Sarah Ainslie studied
photography at Derby College
of Art and has since worked as
a freelance photographer in
London. She mainly does stills
for theatre and television. In
some cases, the photographs
have become an integral part
of the film. Much of the work
shown here has arisen from
Sarah's experience of working
in the theatre – the mystery
of images, thoughts and words
arising like strange clues in the
darkness. Sarah has also
explored British subjects such
as Arsenal football supporters,
Shoreditch at night and past
and present at Spitalfields.
All of these themes have
featured in exhibitions. Sarah
is currently working on a book
in collaboration with strippers
in East End clubs.

CLAUDE ALEXANDRE

Claude Alexandre is a French photographer who has recently moved from Paris to Seville in Spain. Born in 1940, she discovered photography in 1971 and was soon fascinated by all forms of body representation, including men, women, homosexuals, fetishism, sadomasochism, transvestites, bullfighters and dancers. She has published and exhibited widely and has had nine books published in France, Japan, and Germany. She has also featured in many compilations of leading contemporary photographers.

http://www.photographie.com

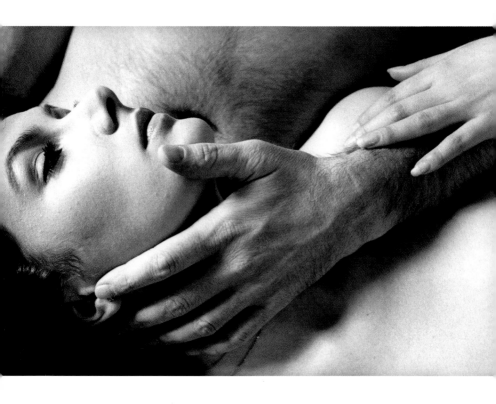

MARC ATKINS

Marc Atkins is a leading
British photographer. Based
in London, he is at the heart
of the Panoptika cooperative,
which also includes Sarah
Ainslie and Françoise Lacroix.
He has been a long-time
collaborator with writer Iain
Sinclair, and his evocative
photographs of buildings,
landscapes and the idiosyncratic
creatures of the British literary
scene have been an integral
part of Sinclair's books. He has
been the subject of many
exhibitions and published
several books, including one
of his nudes. Many of his
images have been used for
book covers and illustrations.

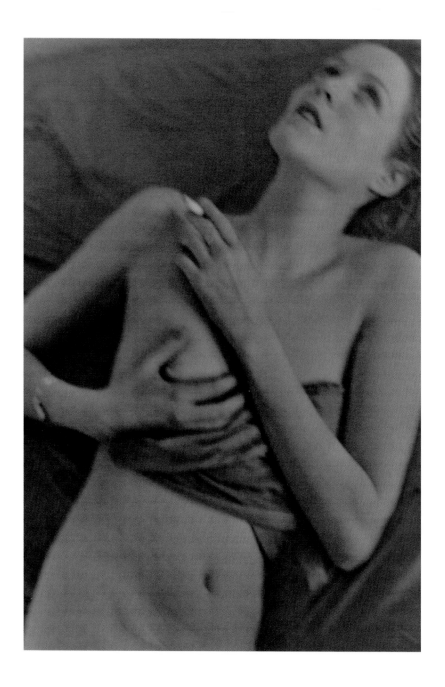

PASCAL BAETENS

Pascal Baetens was born in
Belgium in 1963 in Leuven.
After gaining degrees in
Law and Political and
Social Sciences, he studied
photography in Greece, the
USA and Belgium. He quickly
established himself as a
professional photographer with
his work in fashion, reportage
and travel. His work has often
been published and exhibited,
and featured in some of the
leading books on modern
photography. His portfolios
have also been the subject
of numerous features in
international circles. His solo
books include *The Fragile Touch*
(1999) and *Heavenly Girls*
(2001). He lives in Belgium
and works from his studio
in Kessel-Lo.

http://www.pascalbaetens.com

TREVOR BAKER

Trevor Baker is a Southern
California-based photographer
with a strong interest in fetish
images. He was given his first
camera at the age of eight and
has been shooting ever since.
For many years, photography
was a hobby, but it has been a
full-time occupation for the
past six years. Trevor's work
appears in all the major
magazines in the field and has
been exhibited at various
events and venues. His images
also feature on three websites
and a line of greeting cards
featuring his photos. Books,
CD ROMS and calendars
are being planned.

http://www.fetishimages.com

CARLOS BATTS

Carlos Batts was born in
Baltimore, where he sharpened
his artistic incisors using paint,
lights, props, duct tape and
various other found 'mixed
media'. Now resident in Los
Angeles, his photographs and
artwork have appeared in Dell
Books, DC Comics and many
magazines. He has also directed
adult films and designed for
various punk/hardcore bands.
His first photography book is
published by Editions Reuss.

http://www.cbattsfly.com

PHILIPPE BAUD

Philippe Baud resides in
Kingston, Ontario, where he is
a professional photographer.
Having grown up in the
scenic alpine landscape of
southeastern France, he has
developed a unique portfolio
of nature photography, which,
along with his nude work, has
been published in magazines in
Canada, the USA and France.
He also regularly exhibits in
Kingston and Toronto.

http://www.philippebaud.com

GILLES BERQUET

Gilles Berquet, born in 1956,
lives and works in Paris. He
owns and runs the well-known
erotic art gallery Les Larmes
d'Eros. He has exhibited
worldwide, both as a solo
photographer and as part of
groups. His unique view of
fetishism and the female body
can be witnessed in a number
of books where he treads a thin
line between exhibitionism and
pornography and has been
highly controversial. His
uncompromising glimpse of
extreme fantasy worlds has
won him many admirers as
well as detractors.

MARTIN BOELT

Martin Boelt was born in Germany in 1966 in Lorrach. He graduated as an engineer and later focused on industrial design, photography and video. Since 1992 he has worked as a freelance designer and communication manager in industry. He has also lectured at the Faculty of Product Engineering of the University of Business and Technology of Furtwangen. An autodidact, he enjoys using modern digital media to express eroticism in design, albeit in a strongly classical mode. To his mind, the origin of any erotic spell lies in the eyes of the beholder.

http://martinboelt.de

KEVIN BREAUX

Kevin Breaux was born in
Pennsylvania where he still
resides. He had initial
ambitions to be a comic book
artist and studied at Bucks
County Community College,
where he did all the arts
except photography. He later
transferred to the Tyler Art
School of Temple University
and took his first steps in
photography. He continues
to develop his love and
enchantment for the female
form, moving on from his
original treatments in drawing,
sculpting and comic book
form. He graduated with a
BFA in photography.

ADAM BUTLER

Adam Butler is a British fine
art photographer based in
the very centre of London.
Apart from his work as a
photographer, he is the
co-author of the bestselling
The Art Book. His photographs
are featured in numerous
private collections throughout
Europe and America.

http://www.adambutler.com

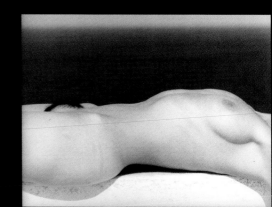

Bob Carlos Clarke

Bob Carlos Clarke was born in southern Ireland in 1950. He came to England in 1964 and eventually studied art and design at the West Sussex College of Art where his interest in photography began. He followed this with three years at the London College of Printing and completed his studies at the Royal College of Arts in 1975. He has established himself as one of the uncontested champions of the art of erotic photography and has been published and exhibited worldwide. His books include *The Illustrated Delta of Venus* (1979), *Obsession* (1981), *The Dark Summer* (1985), *White Heat* (with chef Marco Pierre White, 1990), *Insatiable* (2001) and *Shooting Sex*.

http://www.bobcarlosclarke.com

MIKE CRAWLEY

Mike Crawley was born in
Kent, England in 1950. He
began taking photographs at
the age of seven, when his
parents bought him a Kodak
Box Brownie. He studied
chemistry at Leeds and
Manchester universities and
then worked for Kodak as a
chemist. When career boredom
rekindled his interest in
photography, he attended
evening portrait classes.
Over the last twelve years
he has established himself
as a particularly sensuous
photographer of the female
form. For Mike, the presence
and absence of light, in the
guise of subtle shadows and
patterns, and the contours
of the female body are an
unbeatable combination for
his artistic impression.

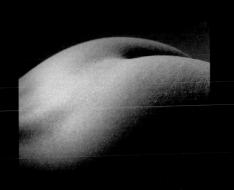

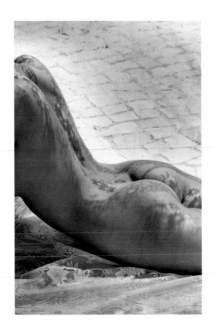

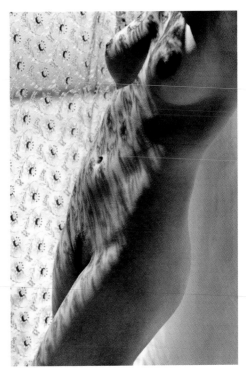

JOHN DIETRICH

John Dietrich was born in
1957, and lives in Birmingham,
England. He developed an
interest in photography in
his early twenties. Drawing
inspiration from George
Hurrell and his friend the late
Terence Donovan he began
working in fashion and beauty
with work for English Vogue.
In 1989 he won the Ilford
Award both as photographer
and printer. His work has been
seen in countless magazines
and books, including much
work in the rock and roll field
and bestselling calendars.
Retrospectives of his work
have been seen in art
galleries internationally.

WOLFGANG EICHLER

Wolfgang Eichler was born in 1954 in Germany. Following studies in psychology and pedagogy, he worked as an art therapist in various hospitals. He studied photography from 1986 to 1991, and began a career as a freelance commercial photographer. He has been published worldwide, and has had a solo exhibition at Cologne's Kunsthaus. He is also the author of two books of nudes: *Liberation* (1993); and *Erotic Photographs* (1995). He has also produced several CD-ROMS about body control, fetishism and domination.

TIM FAIRFIELD

Tim Fairfield lives in
Hamilton, Ontario, Canada.
He is the photographer and
owner of his own company,
Eye Trip Photography. He
first ventured into erotic
photography in 1990 and has
followed a self-taught trial and
error path since. Most of his
photos concentrate on the
beauty of individual body areas
and different perspectives of
the body. In recent years, all his
images have been developed in
the 'digital darkroom', creating
photos that have become some
of his proudest work.

http://www.eyetrip.homestead.com

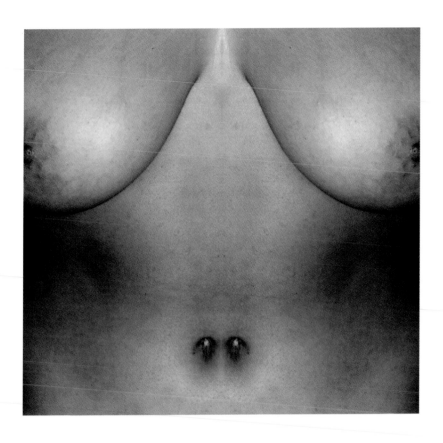

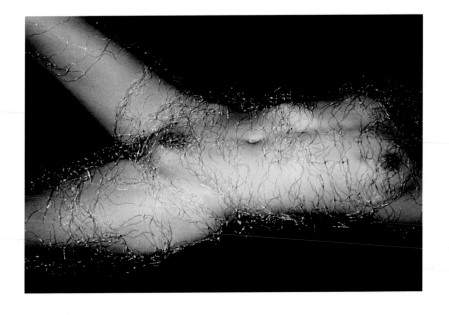

Jody Frost

Jody Frost began in
photography as a model.
Time on the other side of
the lens helped form her ideas
and she began to experiment
with self-portraits. Involved
in dance, she is drawn by
movement and the form and
expression of the human body.
She finds the process of
photographing herself intuitive
and, like others, her desire is to
capture and freeze in a frame
that elusive 'something', that
pure essence of 'thing' that tells
the whole story, animates the
flesh. She has been widely
exhibited in galleries and
museums in New Mexico.

http://www.houseofdreamz.com

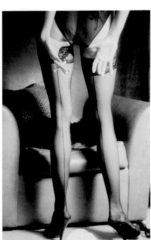

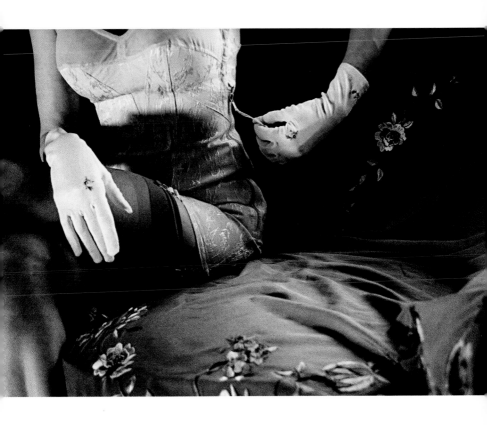

ROGER GAESS

Roger Gaess is a New York
photojournalist who
concentrates on Middle East
affairs. His images have
appeared in a variety of
periodicals. He also does dance
photography and is interested
in 'outsiders' in general.
Erotica - nudes, fetish, alternative
lifestyles - is at the core of his
photographic interests, where
form and its emotional
overtone are a driving force.
Some of his work has appeared
in *Skin Two*. He enjoys
collaborative relationships with
models, in order to explore
ideas and feelings.

aqaba9@aol.com

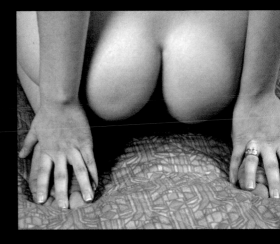

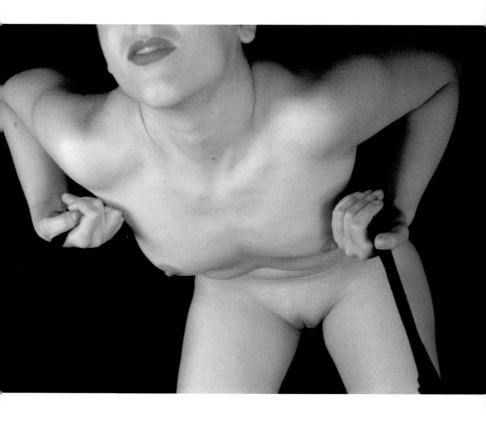

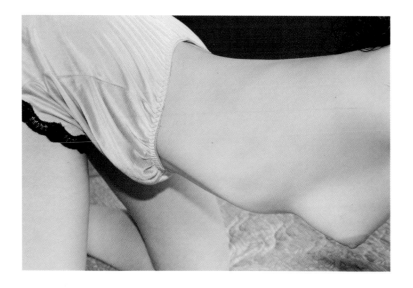

CHARLES GATEWOOD

Charles Gatewood is the
Walker Evans of the sexual
revolution. For more than
30 years his photographs have
probed the darkest corners of
New York and San Francisco's
erogenous zones. A schooled
anthropologist, he is naturally
curious about aberrant
cultures; a non-conformist
himself, he is always willing
to 'join the dance', the better
to understand his subjects.
'Are there still areas of the
behavioural map marked
unknown?' he asks. 'If so, book
my passage at once.' His career
retrospective book *Badlands*
appeared in 2000 and is an
indispensable addition to
any erotic shelf.

http://www.charlesgatewood.com

STEVE DIET GOEDDE

Steve Diet Goedde is a Los Angeles-based, self-taught erotic photographer who has made himself a name by going against the traditional clichés of erotic photography. While most others explore nude landscapes, Goedde prefers to survey the sensual appeal of fetishism. Lovingly documenting such textures as latex, PVC and leather, he manages to remind us that there are people under the clothing. He refuses to pursue photography commercially and only does photography for himself on his own terms. His hardcover retrospective books, *The Beauty of Fetish* and *The Beauty of Fetish: Volume 2* are major publications in the field.

http://www.stevedietgoedde.com

MICHAEL GRAPIN

Michael Grapin was born in
1955 in Jersey City. He was
given his first camera, a Kodak
Instamatic, at the age of eight.
He soon discovered that he
could get people to do
interesting and amusing things
simply by pointing his camera
in their direction. Later, he
found he could get them to
also disrobe and uncovered
many an exhibitionist lurking
within a conservative façade.
So, a hobby may yet lead to a
vocation... as long as he doesn't
have to point his Nikon at any
more weddings or babies!

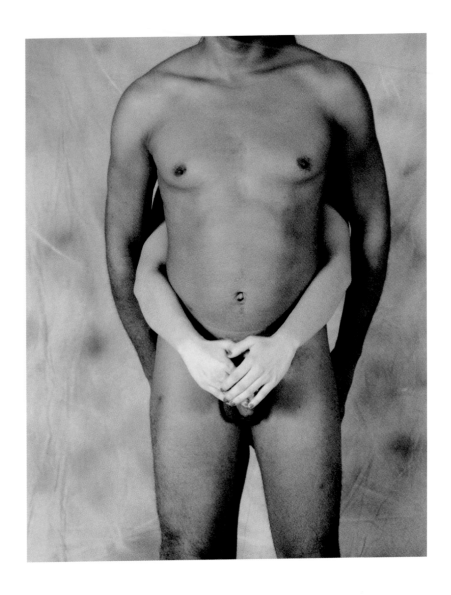

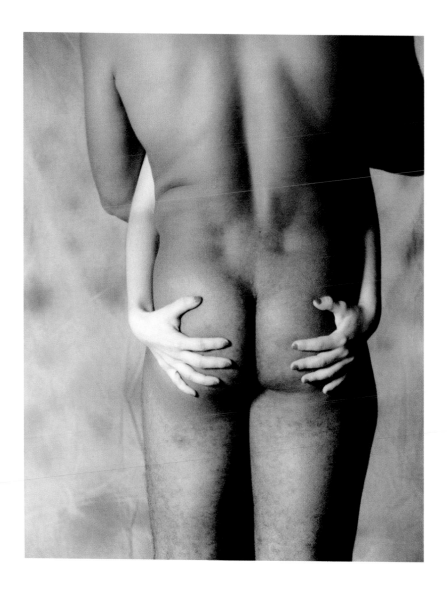

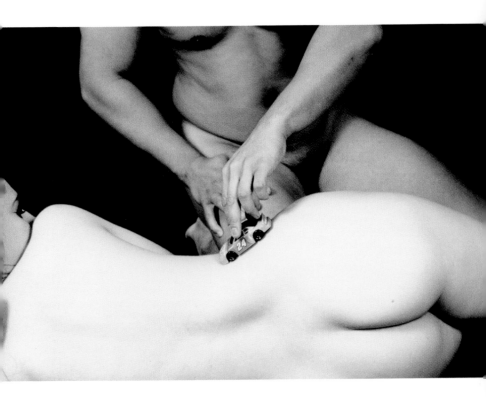

CHINA HAMILTON

China Hamilton is one of
the UK's leading erotic
photographers, with seminal
work in the much-lamented
Journal of Erotica and a
deserving winner of the Erotic
Oscar. His carefully designed,
elaborate work has all the
finesse of Oriental graphics and
a strong strain of old-fashioned
voyeurism that can both
titillate and disturb. A master
of tone, some of his best work
appears in his book, *Woman*, in
which he reveals that '...[his]
job is to touch the mind... even
the heart but not the genitals'.
He is also the rare author of
powerful erotic stories, one of
which appears in *The Mammoth
Book of Erotica*.

PETTER HEGRE

Petter Hegre is a Norwegian
photographer who has worked
as an assistant to Richard
Avedon and studied at Brooks
Institute of Photography in
Santa Barbara, California. He
began photographing his wife
from the day he met her in
1996. He was immediately
smitten and has now taken
more than 6000 pictures of her
and their private life at its most
intimate and indiscreet. His
book *My Wife* has been a
bestselling sensation and is
also, he feels, one of the
most honest books around.
It was the subject of a major
exhibition in Hamburg. He
has now begun another
long-term project with a
young Russian model.

BENJAMIN HOFFMAN

Benjamin Hoffman is based in
Los Angeles where he shares a
studio with his cat, Midnight.
Most of his work has been in
fetish photography, where he
finds black-and-white
timeless. He finds this is a world
that demands mystery, for it is a
world often kept secret. A place
that many people think of as
smudgy and dark, but that he
perceives as quite beautiful. At
times, his own shadows appear
in the images, making this his
most personal photography.

http://www.benjaminhoffman.com

S. D. HOLMAN

Shaira Holman is a professional artist, actor and photographer. Born in Los Angeles, she moved to Canada in 1981. A graduate of the Emily Carr Institute of Art and Design in 1991, Shaira has been a member of important art groups and her work has been shown in a variety of museums and galleries. She has been a regular on the television series *Madison* and performed in many plays. Her renowned photo art exhibition G.I.D... Gender Identity Disorder or Girls in Drag was shown at the Public Library in San Francisco in 2001 following successful shows in Canada.

http://www.elainemiller.com/sdholman

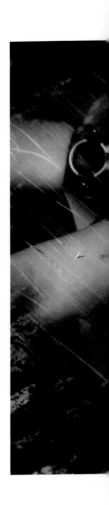

R. C. HORSCH

R.C. Horsch has followed a
life of dissipation as an artist,
filmmaker, composer, writer,
drug smuggler and sometimes
sociopath and years in exile in
New Zealand and Australia.
He made his name with
1960s magazine layouts
which juxtaposed high-fashion
models against skid row
backgrounds. Following
pioneering work for the
Children's Television Workshop,
he produced several low-
budget films and, since 1993,
ground-breaking erotic
documentaries. He lives
in Pennsylvania.

http://www.eroto.com

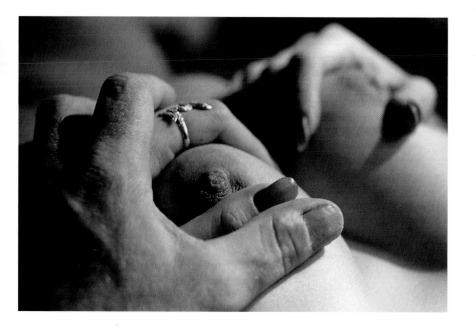

BILL HUDSON

Bill Hudson is a North
Carolina-based American
photographer who was born
in 1960. He purchased his
first camera, a Canon A1 in
Phoenix, Arizona in 1987, and
took thousands of slides on
weekend trips to the Grand
Canyon, Sequoia and Yosemite.
It was then a natural
progression to reading how-to
magazines and investigating
photography seriously. He
acknowledges the important
influence of Alfred Stieglitz.
He still photographs scenes
and landscapes, but portraits
and nudes now dominate
his interests. He jests that his
images are of others, but there
is a lot of him in them, too.

LAURIE JEFFREY

Laurie Jeffrey is a British
photographer. He specialises
in black-and-white portraits
and works from his home and
studio in Lancashire. He began
more than fifteen years ago as a
fashion photographer in
New York and then London,
concentrating on advertising,
figure, fashion, beauty and
travel photography. He spends
about three months each year
shooting on location in Europe
and the Philippines. His wife
Vicky also happens to be
his favourite model. He is
currently working on a major
book project, *Bodyscape*, for
which he has already
accumulated more than
2,000 images.

http://www.ljp.co.uk

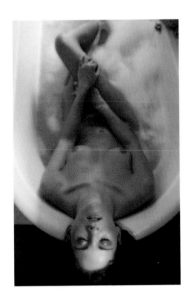

CHAS RAY KRIDER

Chas Ray Krider is a
Columbus, Ohio-based
American fine art and
commercial photographer.
He has attained an awesome
reputation for his ambiguous
and fascinating work in the
fetish glamour field. The
images presented here are from
a body of work entitled *Motel
Fetish* (which already has
forty rooms completed and
mapped), some of which has
appeared in *Pure Magazine*.
The work evokes noir antics
of the 1950s with humour
and voyeuristic glee.

http://motelfetish.com

Françoise Lacroix

London-based Françoise Lacroix graduated in printmaking and photo media from Central St Martins College of Art. She then took a Masters degree in photography at the Royal College of Art. She has exhibited in London, Paris, Berlin and New York.

She and her work have featured in Chris Petit's Channel 4 award-winning film *The Falconer*. Her photos have also been included in several books. Françoise's photography explores the relationship of the body to specific environments.

JACK R. LINDHOLM

Jack R. Lindholm is a photographer and multimedia artist. Originally from the Midwest, he found his way to Gotham City, where he has lived for the last eighteen years. He spent his early years working with photographers such as Irving Penn and Sheila Metzner, and created advertising material for international brands. In his work, he seeks an elusive, intimate place and moment. Fascinated with human beauty and eroticism, he searches for that quiet place where it is found. He succeeds in giving a timeless quality, a feeling of place only imagined and a relationship with his viewer that can only be experienced through his images.
http://divaerotic.com

NIC MARCHANT

Nic Marchant was born in
1962 and picked up a camera
at the tender age of twelve. He
trained as a lighting designer
in theatre. He prefers black-
and-white photography, using
shadows, form and texture.
His work includes many book
covers for leading publishing
houses. He has also built up
strong ties with the company
Skin Two and enjoys working
in the fetish world. He is best
known for his toned
black-and-white images using
chemicals to alter the colour
and composition of prints,
creating one-off originals.

http://www.nicmarchant.co.uk

MAURIZIO MAURI

Maurizio Mauri is an Italian photographer who has made a speciality of capturing the beauty of the female form against the natural beauty and ruins of ancient Rome. He also creates elegant images under the gaze of studio lights, where his mastery of shades of black and white comes spectacularly to the fore.

http://mmf.phidji.com

AERIC MEREDITH-GOUJON

Aeric Meredith-Goujon was raised in southern Indiana. He studied music and creative writing as an undergraduate at Indiana University. He took up photography towards the end of his studies there. After a period of self-study in Paris, he moved to New York City where he received an MFA in photography from the Pratt Institute. He now lives and works in Brooklyn with his wife and daughter.

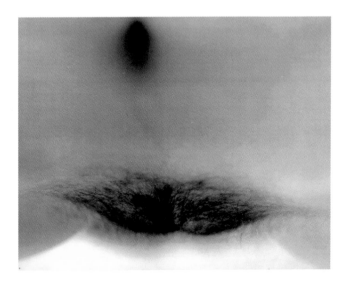

CRAIG MOREY

Craig Morey was born in
1952 in Ft. Wayne, Indiana. He
studied at Indiana University
with noted Bauhaus artist
Henry Holmes Smith. In 1974,
he moved to California where
he and a group of other young
artists founded San Francisco
Camerawork, the first non-
profit photography centre on
the West Coast. His early work
won several prizes, and in 1981
he began a freelance career,
which has seen him published
widely and led him to being
called 'the E.J. Bellocq of
the 1990s'. His book *Studio
Nudes* was published in
1992, followed by *Body
Expression/Silence* in 1994 and
Linea in 1996. His latest project
is *20th Century Studio Nudes*,
publication 2001.

http://www.moreystudio.com

R.F. MORTON

R.F. Morton is an American photographer known for his interpretive work. His haunting imagery is designed to draw the viewer into the scene so as to complete the viewer's own conjecture and emotion. His unique blend of visual elements and themes portrays the more subtle personal interactions and intuitive aspects of fetish and erotica.

rfmorton@editioninternational.com

CHRISTOPHE MOURTHE

Christophe Mourthe is a leading French glamour photographer. Born in 1959, his career began at 20 as a theatre and music hall photographer. Initially inspired by directors like Peter Brook, Franco Zefferelli and Frederico Fellini, he later met make-up and hair styling genius Denis Menendez, and together produced the famous Casanova series, still considered by many as a lasting photographic masterpiece. He has since covered fashion and photographed many film stars. In 1991, he began to explore the world of X-rated film and has since immortalized many of its proponents. The author of a series of bestselling books, he is now planning to shoot his first feature film.

HANS PETER MUFF

Hans Peter Muff is a Swiss
photographer and film-maker
based in Luzern. His first
exhibition was in 1983 at
the Nikon Gallery in Zurich.
His film work has since been
shown at festivals in Tokyo,
Berlin, Zagreb and
Switzerland, including
experimental shorts
*Intermezzo, Einschnitt,
Spiegelbilder, Une Tranche de
Vie* and *Sequenza*. He enjoys
experimenting with all
forms of new techniques
and material. He is currently
working on a project
called *Bondage*.

http://www.muff.buz.ch

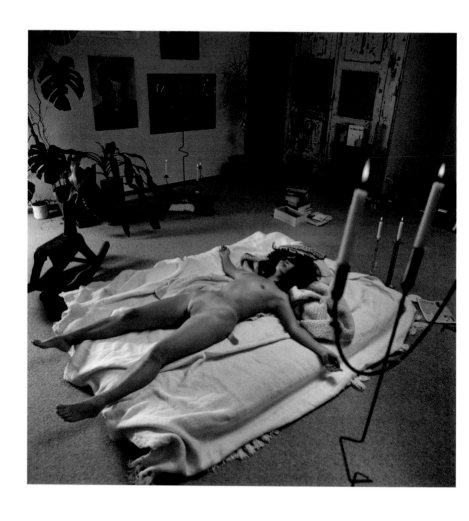

Anja Muller

Anja Muller was born in 1971 in Berlin, Germany. She specializes in erotic photography and portraits. She has been the subject of several exhibitions and been extensively published in Germany. She has authored three books: *Schonner Kommen-Das Lesbensex Buch* (2000), *Frauen* (2000) and *Mannen* (2001). She focuses on the world of gay women and men.

diefotografin@yahoo.de

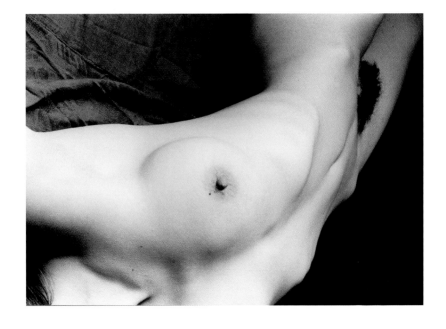

NICHOLAS

Nicholas is a British photographer who still remembers his first picture, taken on an old Kodak Box Brownie given to him by relatives. It was much later, however, that he took a stronger interest in the art, and began developing his own black-and-white film in 1970. For many years, his photography was a private endeavour, an aide-memoire to record the entrances and exits in his life and travels. The photographs collected here are of an almost ethnographic nature, à la E.J. Bellocq's Storyville red-light portraits. It features prostitutes who posed for him in South American brothels. The images convey both the power of witness and the effect their environment has on his subjects. They prove quite memorable as well as erotic in a tender manner.

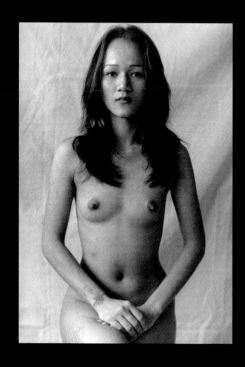

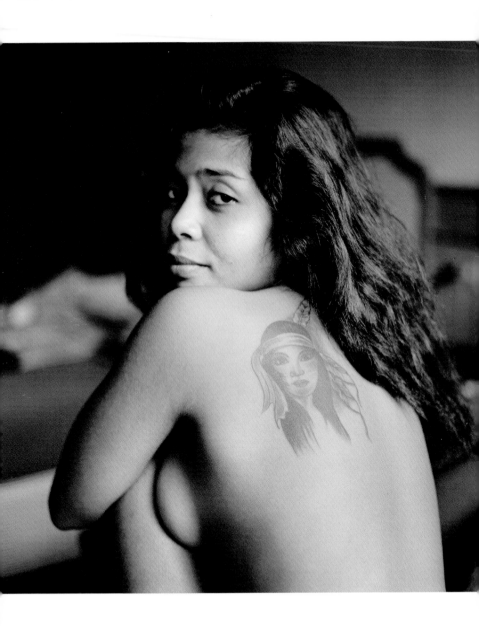

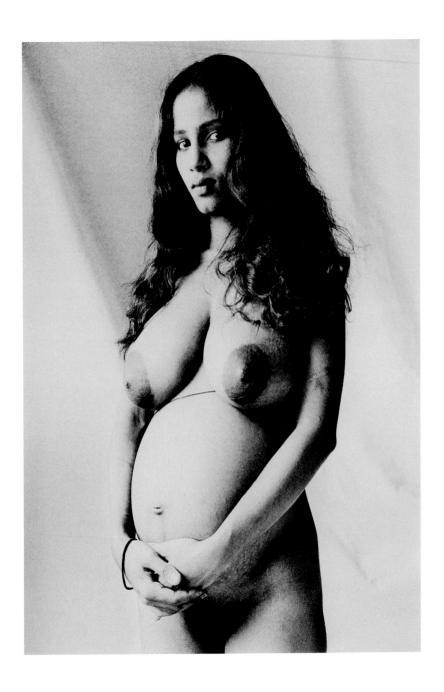

MARC ODLEY

Marc Odley is a British photographer who lives outside Oxford with his wife and two children. He took up photography as a hobby 15 years ago. His first professional position was as a partner for an aerial photography sales company, which involved hanging out of a helicopter at 1500ft with a telephoto lens.

He moved on to newspaper features in sports, beauty and fashion. His career took off in 1994 when he was asked to compile a corporate calendar in fine art nude style. His work has featured on the BBC and in videos. Books and exhibitions are planned for the future.

MIKHAIL PALINCHAK

Mikhail Palinchak was born in
1959 in Uzhgorod, Ukraine.
Photography became his
passion at the age of 12. Most
of his craft has been self-taught
from journals available in the
old USSR. His work has been
shown in more than 300
exhibitions across the world.
He works as a professional
photojournalist for a regional
newspaper. He specializes in
portraits and landscapes. He has
a strong attraction to capturing

JORGE PARRA

Jorge Parra was born in
Caracas, under the sign of
Scorpio. He is self-taught,
but has taken workshops in
New York to complete his
photographic education. He
was employed for some years as
a chemist while publishing his
photos in small publications.
A contract with the fashion
world meant that he could
leave his day job. He now
works mainly in advertising.
His work, including his nudes,
has been use to promote a
wide variety of well-known
brands including Christian
Dior, Seagram, Pepsi Cola,
L'Oreal, Avon Cosmetics and
Procter and Gamble.

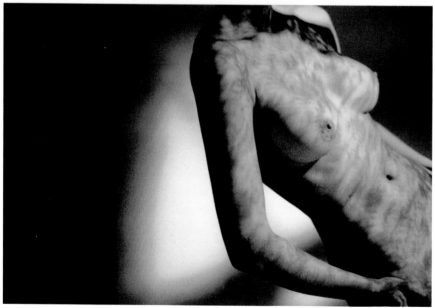

MICK PAYTON

Mick Payton has been a full-time professional photographer for nearly seven years. His first pictures were for a model who wanted a new look. He has since worked on model portfolios, music and commercial contracts while steadily developing his black-and-white body imagery in international markets. Much of his work has been featured on television in Germany and Austria, as well as magazines in England and Austria. His strong and sensual images have also been exhibited in major private art galleries.

http://mickpaytonerotic.com

BRIAN PETERSON

Brian Peterson took his
inspiration from seeing the
work of David Hamilton.
A relative newcomer to
photography, he now balances
this with a career in the world
of computers. Being an
apartment dweller, he
immediately started down the
digital route, bypassing the dark
room and scanning his black-
and-white negatives and
chromes. He focuses on three
themes: the nude in nature; the
nude in the wasteland; and the
beauty of the female form in
the studio.

JEFFERSON POWERS

Jefferson Powers was born in 1972 on an army base in Aurora, Colorado. He began his interest in the arts as an aspiring comic book artist. This led to an interest in painting and graphic design. Jefferson received a degree in Design from the Metropolitan State College of Denver in 1996. It was here that he developed an attraction to photography, that has since eclipsed his other endeavours (although he still paints from time to time). He currently divides his time between shooting nudes in his home studio and operating a comic book store in Colorado.

http://www107.pair.com/jpowers /photo

ELIZABETH PROUVOST

Elizabeth Prouvost has been a
director of cinematography in
the film industry since 1984.
She has worked on many
television features, publicity
spots and promotional clips,
and won the Special Camera
d'Or award at the Cannes Film
Festival in 1990 for her work
on *Farendj*. She diversified into
photography in 1994, and held
her first exhibition in that year.
Many others have followed.
Her first book, *Edwarda*, based
on the Georges Bataille novel,
was published in 1966. For this
project she took more than
3000 photos of her model
Danae, to keep only 33 (the
age of Christ) at the end. Her
latest photographic project,
Transesparence, is influenced by
Francis Bacon and Caravaggio.
She lives in Paris.

HOUSK RANDALL

Housk Randall is an American photographer. He has been long established in Britain, where he has made a mark on the fetish scene with his memorable portraits of denizens of the S/M underworld. Born in 1951, he has also worked as a psychotherapist. His photos have been exhibited in galleries in the UK, Holland, Germany, Norway, the USA and Japan. His fascination for the extremes of body modification has resulted in a series of striking books, some in collaboration with author Mark Ramsden, including *Ritual of Love* (1994) and *The Customised Body* (1996).

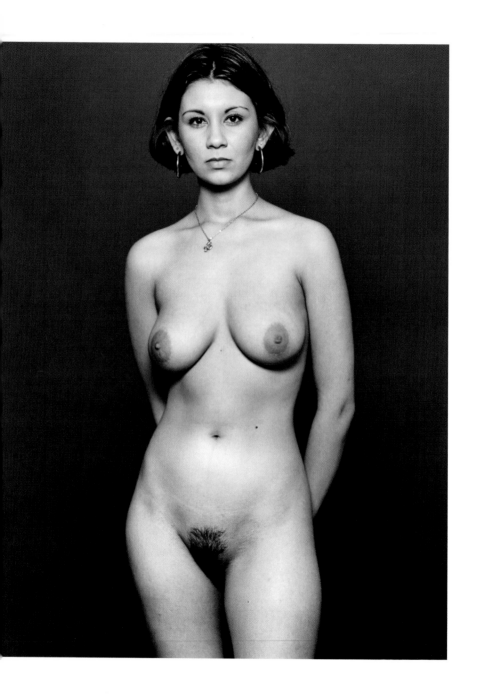

CAT DE RHAM

Cat de Rham is 30 years old, of American-Swiss descent, but her true nationality is nomadic. Born in Malaysia in 1970, she spent most of her childhood exploring the Southeast Asian waters with her parents and younger brother. At fourteen, she left the East to continue her education in Switzerland and then at Brown University in the USA, where she majored in Comparative Literature. She then moved to Italy where she discovered photography. She has never looked back. She has exhibited widely in America and Europe and been published in the world's top photographic magazines and several books, including her own *The Yoga Journey*. She is also a practitioner and teacher of yoga. She lives in London with her husband.

GABRIELE RIGON

Gabriele Rigon is an Italian photographer who also works as a helicopter pilot for the United Nations forces in Lebanon. His passion is for portrait and fine art nude photography, although he has also taken reportage photographs on poverty and deprivation in Africa. The aesthetic form of the female body inspires him and allows his mind to go free when he is shooting. For him, eroticism is much more than nakedness.

http://www.isa.it/rigon

KEVIN ROBERTS

Kevin Roberts was born in
1957 in Springfield, Virginia.
After accumulating a record
number of college credits
including theatre arts, dance,
computer science, maths and
physics, he went in search of a
career and, in 1988, bought a
camera. He progressed through
self-education, families, friends
and girlfriends. He now lives
on the Space Coast of Florida
where he fights local nudity
laws with his love for art and
the human form in an area
where even a thong bikini
is against the law.

http://intimateimages.net

CHARLES ROFF

Charles Roff was born near Inverness in Scotland and was brought up in Rhodesia and Iran. He studied film and photography at Nottingham. He exhibited worldwide between 1977 and 1990 and set up a company to publish posters and postcards. He also established a gallery in Covent Garden. These activities were the subject of a television documentary. Later activities include portraiture, landscapes and nudes for the National Trust and a series of nudes on Cornwall beaches. In 1994, he went to Bosnia as a stills photographer for the BBC. Much of his work there has been used for fundraising for children and the reconstruction

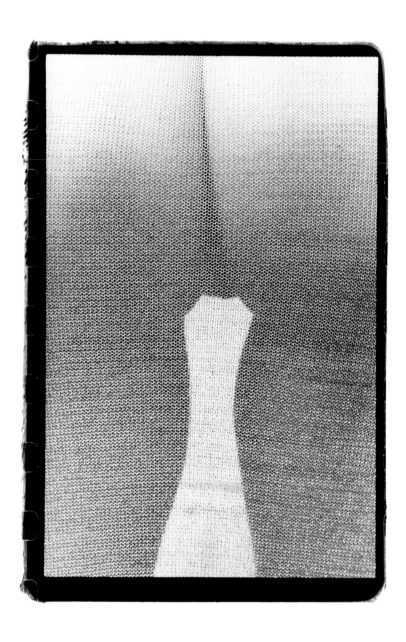

MICHAEL ROSEN

Michael Rosen has been doing sexual photography in San Francisco since 1977. He has documented the sexual revolution in all its myriad forms: stark and grainy nude landscapes; impressionistic, gritty cinema verité images of S/M sex scenes; sharply-focused, elegantly composed, studio sexual portraits involving S/M, erotic piercings, gender play and what he calls non-standard penetration (involving in one instance a regular contributor to the *Mammoth Books of Erotica* series!). A recipient of the Venus Award, Rosen has published several books: *Sexual Magic* (1986), *Sexual Portraits* (1994), and *Lust and Romance* (1998). The photographs in this book are from the late 1970s and published for the first time. *http://www.michaelrosen.com*

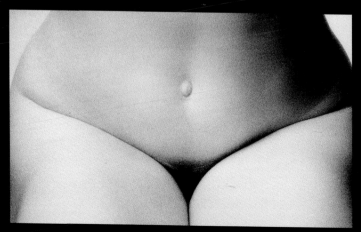

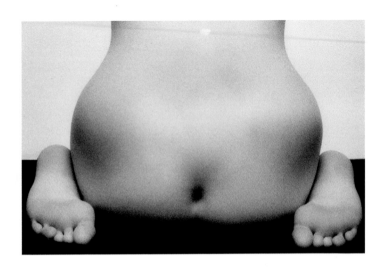

CHRISTER ROSEWELL

Christer Rosewell was born in Sweden. He likes to provide a unique medium and transcendental blend of images based on his years of experience and a deep respect for the masters of his trade. Between the black and the white come many shades of grey, and it is in that zone that the emotions dance and eroticism can be found in his subjects. From shots when the viewers are brought into the frame and the very moment when beauty is captured, to direct classical images where form is transformed into art, Christer's work provides an opportunity to be safe and in love.

http://ChristerArt.com

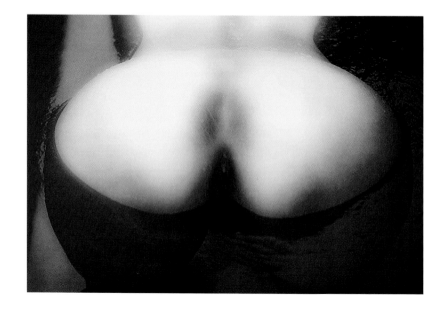

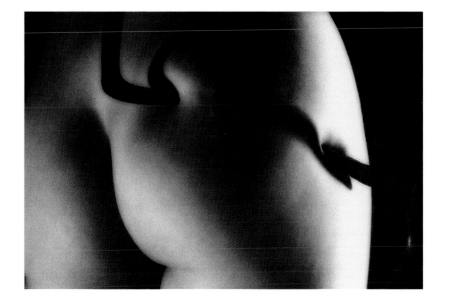

MAURICE SALMON

Maurice Salmon was born in 1943 in Bievres, France, close to the Museum of Photography. Maurice is an electronics engineer by training, but the photographic arts have run for generations through his family. He began taking pictures of his children and places seen on his holidays. He then moved on to taking images of artistic sports like skating and dance. The female body remains his passion, not as a form of aesthetic research but as a way to express emotions and fantasies. His work has appeared in many magazines (including *Photo*) and dance publications, and he has had several solo shows in galleries.

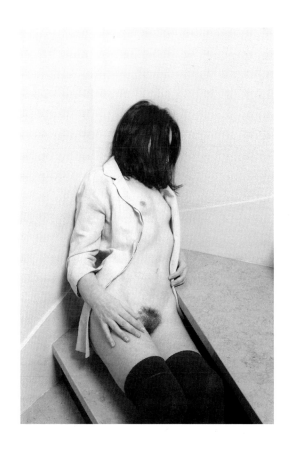

MARCO SANGES

Marco Sanges was born in Rome in 1970. For many years, he worked as a lab developer of black-and-white photos. He then collaborated for a lengthy period with Italian Vogue and other leading magazines. Following work in Rome and Milan, Marco moved to London in 1996.

He has since contributed to many leading newspapers and magazines and had several exhibitions. For him, each photo has to tell a story, a 'play of life' between old and new, darkness and light, dreams and reality, often inspired by black-and-white films from the 1920s and 1930s.

JOHN SANTERINEROSS

John Santerineross has a
unique style and palette of
erotic imagery. While he is
technically a photographer
due to his use of photographic
materials, he considers himself
more of an image-maker.
Greatly influenced by the
Symbolists, his imagery is
primarily inspired by his
exposure to Catholicism
and Santaria as a child and
a fascination with Greek
mythology and world
symbolism. Although he
uses bondage and S/M
scenarios, he does not see
himself as a fetish photographer
and uses eroticism to explore
boundaries imposed on us
by religion, media and other
societal pressures. His book
Fruit of the Secret God
appeared in 1999.

http://www.attis.nu

CRAIG SCOFFONE

Craig Scoffone has chosen the
human form, and in particular
that of the female nude, as the
common thread throughout
most of his fine art work, with
a choice of techniques,
different lighting, film and
processes always in evolution.
Since 1979, his photos have
been featured in numerous
group shows and solo
exhibitions. They have also
been published internationally
in leading magazines across the
world, including Italy, Spain
and even China, in addition to
publications in the English-
speaking world.

http://www.erotic-fine-art.com

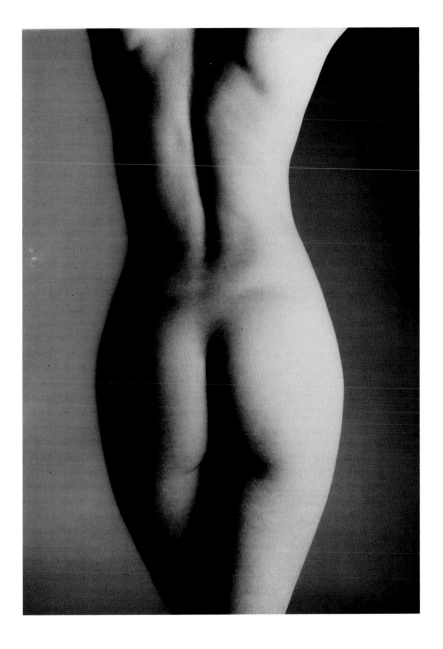

G. SCOTT

G. Scott is a New York
City-based photographer
who focuses on fine arts
photography. After purchasing
his first camera five years ago,
he has been aggressively
pursuing his art ever since.
'I like to experiment with light
to express the reality and
texture of the industrial
environment and highlight the
drama of the human form
within that environment.
I have only begun to explore
the beauty and eroticism that
can be expressed through this
visual medium'.

http://www.IndustrialErotica.com

MICHELE SERCHUK

Michele Serchuk is currently
Photography Associate for
On Our Backs magazine and is
regularly published there and
in *Cupido*. Her work has also
appeared in all the major
magazines in the field and
her cover art used by
publishers in the USA and
England. She seldom uses
professional models, although
some subjects are Dommes or
performers. What they all share
is the desire to take erotic
exploration into a visual realm.
In her work, Serchuk prefers to
follow her models' passions
rather than cast them as people
they are not. They reveal to us
their own personal fascinations,
fetishes and fantasies, and they
are active participants in the
orchestration of the image.

http://www.photodiva.com

CLIFF SIDNELL

Cliff J. Sidnell was born in London in 1956 and moved to Essex/Suffolk borders in 2000 for a less stressful environment to concentrate on photography and writing. Passionate about erotic art imagery, black-and-white in particular, he also likes to experiment with coloured black and white images for a different approach. He was first published in 1992 in *Black and White Art Photographer* magazine and has since been published widely in the UK and Europe.

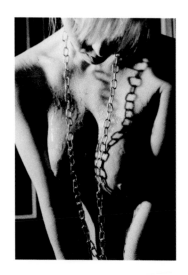

DAVID STEINBERG

David Steinberg is a sexual
campaigner from Santa Cruz,
California, well known for his
authoritative and controversial
newsletter *Comes Naturally*, in
which he ably dissects the
sexual mores of society and
the world today. Fascinated
by the dynamics of sexual
photography, he likes to work
with couples in loving
relationships in the familiarity
of their own homes. He is
interested in models of all ages,
genders, ethnicities and sexual
orientations, strongly believing
that sex is not reserved for the
young, thin, glamorous people
we see in mainstream media.

eronat@aol.com

JULIE STRAIN

Julie Strain is of course better-
known for her career as scream
movie actress and sculptural
model. But photography is
now her game. She has spread
her legs and posed herself but
those days will soon be on the
shelf. There is a magic, she
feels, in creating celluloid. In
her life it has filled quite a vast
void. Having given up make-
up and false eye-lashes, she will
now shoot other women. She
will still do some movies and
pose, since she likes to see
herself everywhere but, as as
lensman, she promises to be
all the rage!

ROY STUART

Roy Stuart, an American photographer now settled in Paris, is undoubtedly one of the major proponents of modern and disturbing erotic photography. His images and scenarios are like small silent movies enacted for our voyeuristic pleasure and fascination, begging the question of what happened before the shots or might occur afterwards. From city streets with sexy revelations galore to indoor encounters of the sexual kind, his world is one of desire and lust kept under tight control. A regular contributor to the infamous *Leg Show* magazine, much of Roy Stuart's work has been collected in three weighty books from Taschen, all simply bearing his name.

ROGER TASSIN

Roger Tassin is a French photographer. He was born in the Congo in 1956, but moved back to France in 1968. He discovered his vocation at 16 when visiting a photo club with a friend. Following work on landscapes and street scenes, he tried female nudes under the influence of Jean-Loup Sieff and Ralph Gibson. He has now been active for twenty years, taking photographs of close acquaintances with whom he has a sentimental relationship, which show no shames or complexes. His photographs should be viewed as delicious and spicy tastes of good times past and he hopes that viewers will enjoy their pleasure as much as he did.

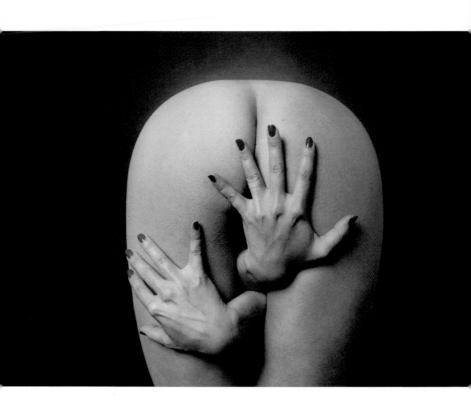

KERRY R. TRACY

Kerry R. Tracy is an American
photographer from Kansas. He
was a freelance artist before
switching to photography
and has now practised
professionally for 17 years.
He has moved from portrait
photography to fine art nudes.
Technically self-taught, he
always uses amateur models
and prefers to display a soft,
sensual side of eroticism. His
work can be seen in leading
magazines and websites.

MARC TRAVANTI

Marc Travanti is a New York visual artist whose work has been published in the award-winning *The Erotica Project*, (Cleis Press, San Francisco) and in *New York Newsday*. His paintings, photographs and sculptures have been exhibited in major New York City galleries including The New Museum, Stux Gallery, Jack Tilton and Feature. He holds an MFA from the University of Colorado, Boulder.

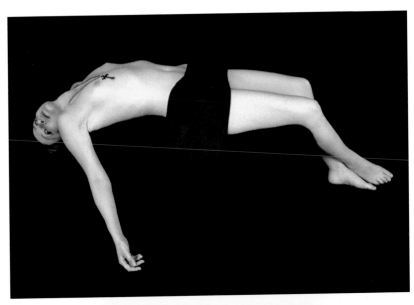

TOHIL TREVINO

Tohil Trevino is a Mexican photographer who lives in Monterrey, Mexico. Previously a student of architecture, he began a career as a commercial photographer in 1996. A co-founder of La Maquina de Foto, a photographic agency, he combines his passions for photography and the female body. He usually prefers to shoot friends rather than professional models, which he finds makes the sessions more comfortable and relaxed, as well as providing a personal touch to the finished results.

http://www.lamaquinadefoto.com

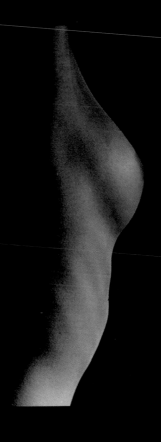

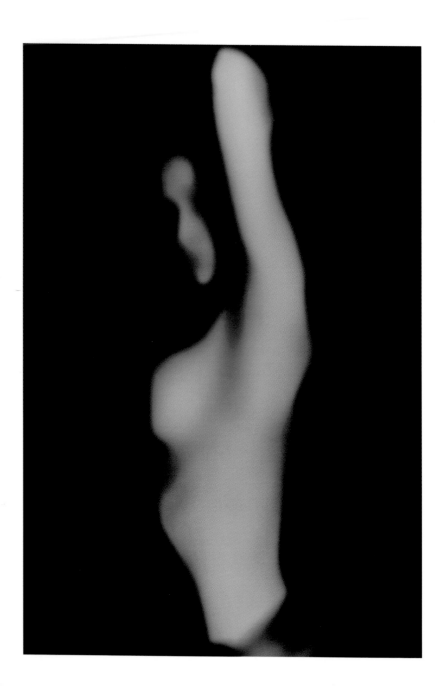

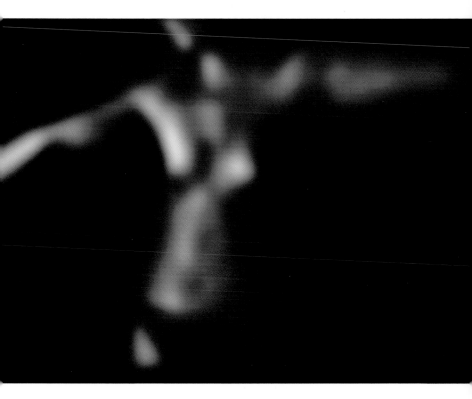

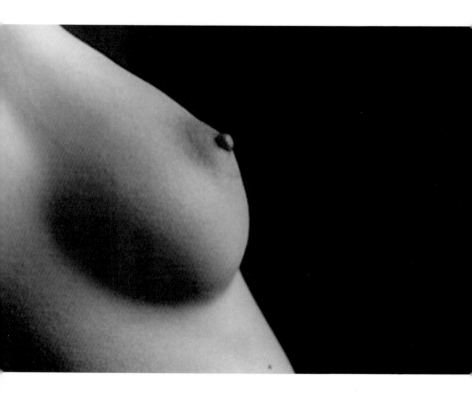

MIKKEL URUP

Mikkel Urup is an award-winning Danish photographer with a major body of work in the field of erotic photography and film, and a big following worldwide. He feels that what describes an artist is the same thing that describes an adventurer. The longing for something intense, grand, revolutionary, with new horizons. He hopes his erotic images can provide a little of that.

http://www.surfersheart.com

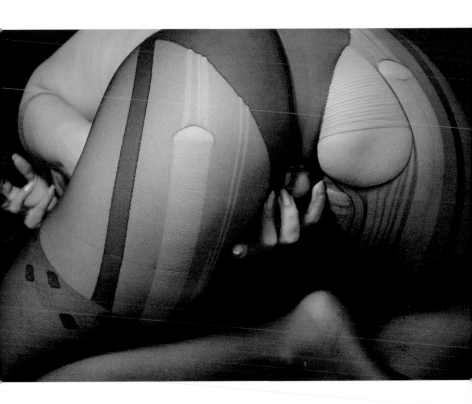

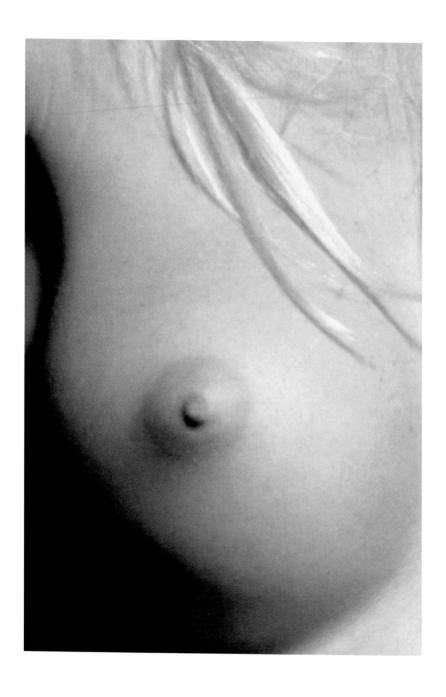

VERETTA

Veretta is a New York-based professional photographer. She has worked in fine arts, fashion and portraiture and still life for twenty years. Her work has appeared in countless magazines and her art photography is part of several private and corporation collections. She grew up in Kansas and has a BSc in photojournalism from the University of Kansas. She has contributed to the book *Gift Of Power*, and produced a 2001 calendar, *The Red Road*, and a greetings card series. She is the President of V Group Advertising Agency, Inc., founded in 1991.

http://www.veretta.com

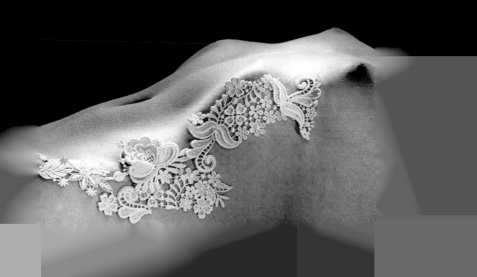

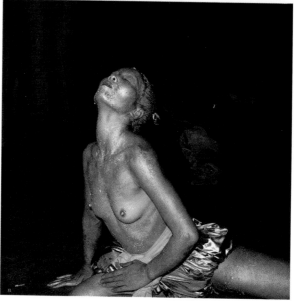

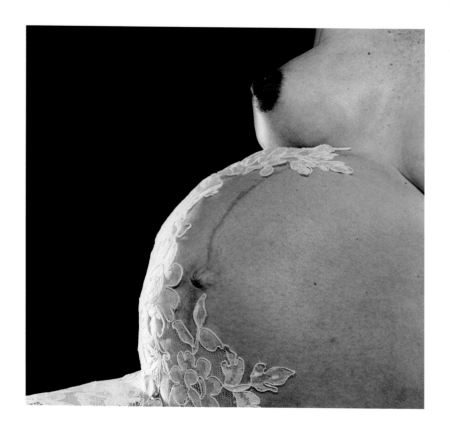

MARC ADRIAN VILLAS

Marc Adrian Villas was born in 1960 in Mexico City to a Mexican painter and an American artist. Following a BA at Mexico University, he edited the magazine *Nosotros* for three years. He then attended the University of Texas at San Antonio, where he studied photography. Marc subsequently moved to New York City, where he completed his studies and began publishing in prestigious magazines. He transferred to Portland, Oregon in 1992, where his photographic career burgeoned. He opened his downtown New York City studio in 1996 and now works on portrait and commercial photography for publications around the world, including the *New York Times* and *Harper's Bazaar*.

http://nyphotostudio.com

TONY WARD

Tony Ward was born in 1955 in Philadelphia and has a degree from Millersville University and a Masters from Rochester Institute of Technology. His erotic photography has been featured in two controversial books, *Obsessions* and *Orgasm,* and exhibited around the world in leading galleries. His fascination with sensuality, beauty and the erotic often borders on the X-rated, but displays a singular and courageous vision, full of daring and taboos. He publishes much of his current work in *Penthouse,* transcending the stigmas that the modern art world often applies to erotica. He lives in Philadelphia with his business partner and their three children.

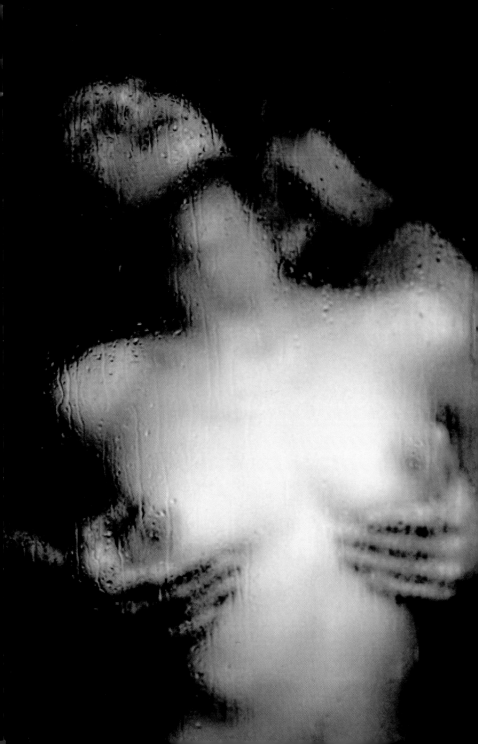

TREVOR WATSON

Trevor Watson is one of
Britain's leading photographers
in the realm of eroticism.
Working with his then partner
Francesca, dancers, artists and
dominatrixes, he quickly
established a strong reputation,
and his work has appeared in
all the major magazines in the
field. His distinctive style
captures like no one else girls
behaving badly. His provocative
and sexy book, *Cheeks,* is an
indispensable addition to any
erotic shelf. He was already
thirty when he first picked up
a camera. He lives in West
London with his partner
Debbie.

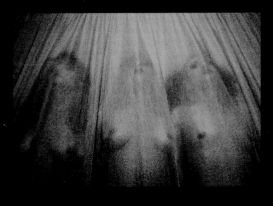

BEN WESTWOOD

Ben Westwood is the son of
notorious couture designer
Vivienne Westwood. He
launched his career in glamour
photography in *Skin Two* in
1993 with portfolios of
modern interpretations of
1950s-style pin-ups. He has
since developed a unique style
of portraying peek-a-boo
lingerie and outré situations
and strong empowered women,
no doubt influenced by his
formative years on the seminal
punk scene. His work has now
appeared both in the glamour
field and high fashion. His first
book, *Ben Westwood*, was first
published in Japan.

JAMES WILLIAMS

James Williams was born and raised in Las Vegas. A father of three, he uses his wife as model in most of his images. He first picked up on the beauty of the female form from Playboy and never knew that one day he'd be shooting nudes himself. Over the last year he has changed his vision of what he wants to shoot and has turned to more artistic work than glamour. His inspirations include Helmut Newton, Mapplethorpe, Demarchelier and various web-based photographers such as Lindsay Garrett, Gennadi and Rob Debenport.

http://www.beauty-nudes.com
http://www.jwilliams-photography.com

HARRY WYNN

Harry Wynn is an American
photographer who, as a child,
was taught that nudity was
basically dirty. He never really
agreed with this logic, because
to him there isn't anything
quite so beautiful. So he will
continue to photograph the
nude until the day he dies. He
was born in Tampa, Florida,
was raised in northeast Ohio
and now lives in Cleveland
with his very large family of
children, step-children and
grandchildren.

http://www.figurefoto.com

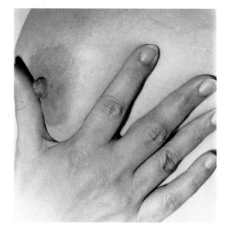